ZUZE AND THE STAR

VICKI C. HAYES

SADDLEBACK
EDUCATIONAL PUBLISHING

red rhino
bOOks™

With more titles on the way …

SADDLEBACK
EDUCATIONAL PUBLISHING
www.sdlback.com

ISBN-13: 978-1-62250-915-7
ISBN-10: 1-62250-915-3
eBook: 978-1-63078-042-5

Printed in Guangzhou, China
NOR/1014/CA21401612

19 18 17 16 15   1 2 3 4 5

ZUZE

Age: just turned 13

Family: has an annoying younger brother

Bedroom Decor: posters of pop stars

Future Goal: to be lead singer in the most famous rock band ever.

Best Quality: quick to forgive

CHARACTERS

Emm

Age: 12

Nickname at School: teacher's pet

Favorite Treat: ice cream truck rocket pops

Wants to Become: a poet and a lawyer and a veterinarian.

Best Quality: very organized

1
CLASS TRIP

It was the year 2143. Zuze was in seventh grade. Today, Zuze was in music class. Zuze loved music. She loved all kinds of music. Her friend was in the class too. Her friend was Emm. The teacher was Ms. Cleff.

"Class, I have some work for you," said Ms. Cleff. "You are going to write a paper. The paper will be about a singer. The singer must be from the past."

Zuze talked softly to Emm.

"I don't like writing papers," Zuze said. Then she raised her hand. "It is hard to write a paper," she told Ms. Cleff. "What do we write?"

"This paper will not be hard," said Ms. Cleff. "You'll see. First you will pick a singer you like. Then you will learn about your singer."

"How will we do that?" asked Zuze.

"We will take a trip," said Ms. Cleff. "It will be a time travel trip."

going back in time!

Many new things had been made by the year 2143. One new thing was time travel. The people in 2143 could travel in time.

Zuze and Emm were excited. This would be their first time travel trip. Zuze raised her hand again.

"Are we going to visit the singers?" she asked.

"Yes," said Ms. Cleff. "We're going back in time. We're going to see singers in the past."

"I love old music," Zuze said to Emm. "I can't wait for this trip." Zuze raised her hand again.

"Who will we see?" she asked Ms. Cleff. Zuze liked one singer the best. She hoped they would visit him.

"We will visit five singers," said Ms. Cleff. "You must tell me the singers you like. Then I will pick five. Those five will be the singers we will visit."

The class was excited. Each kid got a scrap of paper. Each kid wrote a singer's name on the paper. They folded the papers. Then they gave the papers to Ms. Cleff. She put the papers in a box. She shook the box.

Emm looked at Zuze. "I know the name you wrote," she said. "You wrote Rufus Roth."

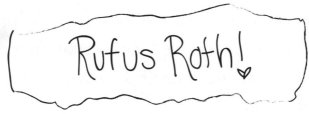

Zuze nodded. "Yes," said Zuze. "Rufus Roth is the best singer ever. He's a star." Zuze really wanted to visit Rufus Roth.

Ms. Cleff put her hand in the box. She grabbed five papers. She took them out. She read each one out loud.

"Bronx Moon," said Ms. Cleff. Some kids cheered. Zuze rubbed her nose.

"Riker 5," said Ms. Cleff. Some more kids cheered. Zuze rubbed her ear.

"Ayza," said Ms. Cleff. Emm cheered. Zuze was happy for Emm.

at least Emm is happy

"Talon," said Ms. Cleff. Lots of kids cheered. Zuze looked sad. She really wanted to visit Rufus Roth. Zuze crossed her fingers. Zuze crossed her arms. Zuze crossed her eyes. Zuze even tried to cross her toes.

Ms. Cleff read the last name.

"Rufus Roth."

Zuze cheered!

2
RULES

Ms. Cleff talked to the class.

"This is your first time travel trip," she said. "Time travel has four rules. Who can tell me the rules?"

Zuze and Emm knew the rules. Everyone knew the rules. Zuze raised her hand.

"Time travel only goes into the past," said Zuze.

Time travel:

"You are right," said Ms. Cleff. "Time travel only works one way. What is rule two?" Jep raised his hand.

"The people in the past can't see us," said Jep.

"Yes," said Ms. Cleff. "No one will see us. We can stand very close. But no one will see us. This will be good at the concerts. We will stand next to the stage. The people will see the singers. They will not see us. It will be fun. What is rule three?" Mat raised his hand.

"We can't change things," said Mat.

"Very good," said Ms. Cleff. "We cannot change the past. Some time travelers try to change things. But nothing happens. Time travelers cannot change the past. But what *can* we do?" Kimmy raised her hand.

"We can watch and listen," said Kimmy.

"We can watch," said Ms. Cleff. "And we can listen. We can watch the singers. We can listen to the songs." Ms. Cleff went to the wall screen.

"You did a good job," said Ms. Cleff. "You knew all the rules. Here they are again." Ms. Cleff put the rules on the wall screen. The class read the rules.

1. Time travel only goes into the past.

2. The people in the past will not see or hear you.

3. Time travelers cannot change anything.

4. Time travelers can watch and listen.

"On our trip you must take notes," said Ms. Cleff. "You will write about the singers. You will write about the concerts. Then we will come home. You will read your notes. You will write your papers. It will not be hard."

"I can't wait," said Zuze. "I can't wait to see Rufus Roth. He is the best singer of all time."

"He is good," said Emm. "But Ayza is good too."

"Ayza doesn't sing the best song," said Zuze. "Only Rufus Roth sings the best song."

"What's the best song?" asked Emm.

"The best song is 'Susie Girl,'" said Zuze. "It's a fun song. I like the jumpy music. I like the happy words. The song is about a cute girl. I bet the girl is Rufus's friend. I bet Susie is Rufus's girlfriend."

"Maybe," said Emm. "Maybe we'll find out on our trip."

3
THE BIG DAY

Soon it was the day of the trip. Zuze was very excited. The class was very excited. Class trips were lots of fun. But a time travel trip would be even more fun.

"Does everyone have a notepad?" asked Ms. Cleff.

Ready to go! →

All the kids checked their packs.

"Make sure your notepad has power," said Ms. Cleff. "You will be taking a lot of notes."

All the kids checked again. Everyone was ready.

"Now let's head out to the zoom bus," said Ms. Cleff. "The zoom bus will take us to the TTC. TTC means Time Travel Center. We will start our trip from the TTC."

"Everyone knows about the TTC," said Zuze. "Why did she say that?"

The ZOOM bus

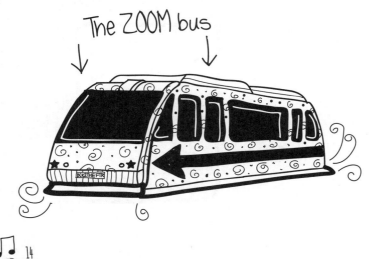

"She is the teacher," said Emm. "Teachers always say things like that."

Zuze laughed. She was in a good mood.

The class headed out to the zoom bus. They climbed aboard. The bus flew them to the TTC. The TTC was a big building. It was tall. It was white. Ms. Cleff and the kids got off the bus. They all went into the TTC.

"This way," said Ms. Cleff. She showed the class a sign. The sign read Time Travel Room.

The class walked down a hall. They

15

walked to the Time Travel Room. There was a new sign. It read School Groups Meet Here.

A man was waiting. He was waiting under the sign. He had on a white shirt. He had on white pants. He had on a name tag. His name was Jiff.

"Welcome," said Jiff. "Welcome to the TTC. This is where your trip starts. Now follow me."

Jiff led the class down a new hall. They went in a big room. There were raised circles on the floor. The circles were white.

"You must each stand on a circle," said

Jiff. "The trip will start soon." Zuze and Emm stood on circles. They stood next to each other.

Jiff went to Ms. Cleff. He showed her a list. It was a list of five dates.

"Are these the dates you want to visit?" asked Jiff. Ms. Cleff checked the list.

Ready or not...

"Yes," she said. "You have the right dates."

"Good," said Jiff. "Is everyone on a circle?" Zuze looked at the other kids. They were standing on circles. Zuze looked at

Emm. She was standing on a circle. She was next to Zuze. Ms. Cleff stood on a circle too. She looked at her class.

"We are ready," said Ms. Cleff to Jiff. "You may start the trip."

Zuze was excited. This was her first time travel trip. Her mom said it would be fun. Her dad said it would be fun. But Zuze was a little scared. She didn't know what it would feel like.

Jiff stood by the wall. There was a screen on the wall. There were buttons on the screen. Jiff held his finger near a button.

"Here you go," said Jiff. He pushed a button.

This way to the past

4
THE TRIP

At first Zuze felt nothing. Then she felt a shake. She felt a shake and a wiggle. Her head felt dizzy. Her eyes went fuzzy. She couldn't see Jiff. She couldn't see Emm. She couldn't see the room. Everything was dim. It was very strange. Zuze closed her eyes.

Feeling DIZZY

Then the shaking stopped. The wiggling stopped. Zuze opened her eyes. She was in a big room. It was not the TTC room. This room looked old. It looked like a room from the past.

"This is the lobby," said Ms. Cleff. "This is where people come in. Then they go into the concert hall." Ms. Cleff pointed at some doors.

"Stay with me," said Ms. Cleff. "We are going into the hall. This is the year 2025. We are going to hear Bronx Moon."

STOP #1:

Ms. Cleff walked to the doors. The class followed her. Ms. Cleff pushed open the doors. She went into the hall. The class went into the hall.

The hall was full of people. The people were sitting. They were listening to the concert. Ms. Cleff led the class to the front of the hall. They stood next to the stage.

Bronx Moon was on the stage. His band was on the stage. He was singing. He was playing a guitar. Zuze didn't look at Bronx Moon. She looked at the people in the seats. Then she talked softly to Emm.

"We are in front of everyone," said Zuze. "The people can't see the stage."

"Yes, they can," said Emm. "They are looking through us. They can't see us."

Zuze looked at the people. Then Zuze waved her hands. But no one looked at her.

"Look at me!" yelled Zuze. The people did not look at her. But Ms. Cleff did.

"Be quiet," said Ms. Cleff. "The class wants to hear the concert."

Zuze turned around. She watched the concert. She listened to Bronx Moon. Then he ended his song. All the people clapped.

All the people cheered. Zuze and Emm clapped too. They clapped and cheered. Everyone in their class clapped and cheered.

Soon Bronx Moon ended a second song. Ms. Cleff looked at her class.

"We are going," said Ms. Cleff. "We are going back to the lobby. It is time for concert number two." The class followed Ms. Cleff. They walked past all the people.

Zuze talked softly to Emm.

"Can I touch these people?" Zuze asked.

Please don't touch the HUMANS!

"No," said Emm. "They can't see us." But Zuze wasn't sure. She walked by a girl with long hair. Zuze flipped the girl's hair. The hair did not move. Zuze walked by a boy with a hat. Zuze pushed on the hat. The hat did not move.

"See," said Emm. "You can't touch them."

"No," said Zuze. "My hands go through them."

The class went back to the lobby. Ms. Cleff had been watching her class. She had been watching Zuze.

"Class," said Ms. Cleff. "Do not touch the people."

"But they can't feel us," said Zuze.

"That's right," said Ms. Cleff. "But there are rules. You must leave the people alone." Zuze nodded. The other kids nodded too.

Then Ms. Cleff pulled out a small pad. It had a screen. The screen had buttons. Ms. Cleff pushed a button.

"I have buzzed Jiff," said Ms. Cleff. "He is sending us to concert number two. Concert number two is Riker 5. Everyone stand still. Here we go."

5
MORE CONCERTS

This time Zuze was not scared. She knew there would be shaking. She knew there would be wiggling. She closed her eyes. But she did not get dizzy.

"Here we are," said Ms. Cleff. "It is 2031. We are at concert number two. This is Riker 5."

#2:

Zuze followed the class into the concert hall. They walked past the people in seats. They walked up to the stage. Riker 5 was on the stage. They were singing. Zuze watched them.

"They are pretty good," Zuze said to Emm. "But they are not Rufus Roth." Zuze took out her pad. She made some notes. The class listened to two songs. Then Ms. Cleff spoke.

"Time for concert number three," said Ms. Cleff. "Talon is next."

"I don't like Talon," said Zuze.

STOP #3: **Talon**

(not excited ↑)

"Me neither," said Emm. "He's too loud."

Ms. Cleff walked back to the lobby. The

class followed her. Some of the kids wrote notes. Ms. Cleff waited for them to finish.

"Is everyone ready?" asked Ms. Cleff. The kids put their notes away. Ms. Cleff pushed the button on her pad. Zuze did not close her eyes. She liked time travel now.

The class went to the Talon concert. Zuze and Emm stood in the back. They did not like Talon. He was loud. His songs were mad. The class listened to two songs. Then it was time to leave. Zuze and Emm were first out of the hall.

"Time for concert number four," said Ms. Cleff. "Ayza is next."

"Good," said Emm. "Ayza is the best."

STOP #4: Ayza

"She may be the best for you," said Zuze. "But I think Rufus Roth is best." Zuze couldn't wait for Rufus Roth.

The class stood in the lobby. Ms. Cleff pushed the button. Everything wiggled, then stopped.

"We're here!" yelled Emm. "Let's go in." Emm went to the doors of the concert hall.

"Wait, Emm," said Ms. Cleff. "We must stay in a group." Emm waited.

"Okay," said Emm. "But I want to be first in the hall."

"This is 2037," said Ms. Cleff. "And we will hear Ayza."

Then the class went in. Emm was next to Ms. Cleff.

"Look!" said Emm. "Look at Ayza." Emm pointed at the stage. Ayza was tall. She had lots of black hair. Her hair sparkled. She had on a long blue dress. Her dress sparkled. Even her shoes sparkled.

← Emm's favorite

Ayza held a mic. She sang a slow song. The song was sad. Then the song ended. The people in the hall stood up. They cheered. They loved the song.

"That was great!" said Emm. "I love that song."

"It's too sad for me," said Zuze. "I like happy songs." Zuze wrote some notes.

Ayza sang one more slow song. Then it was time to go.

"Okay, class," said Ms. Cleff. "We have one last stop. We are going to the year 2040. We are going to hear Rufus Roth."

Zuze couldn't wait.

6
THE STAR

The class arrived in a new lobby. Zuze could hear Rufus Roth. He was singing a good song.

"Let's go in," she said. "Let's go in right now."

"Okay," said Ms. Cleff. "But you must not run. I know you like Rufus Roth. But follow the rules."

Zuze led the class into the hall. She went right up to the stage. She looked at Rufus Roth. He had on white pants. He had on a dark blue shirt. He had long brown hair. He was cute.

33

Zuze watched Rufus Roth sing. He sang a good song. The song had happy words. The people clapped and cheered. Zuze clapped. But she did not cheer. She wanted to hear "Susie Girl."

Rufus Roth sang another song. It was a good song. The song had jumpy music. The people clapped and cheered. Zuze clapped. But Zuze did not cheer.

"Well, what did you think?" asked Emm.

"He is a star," said Zuze. "He is the best of all time."

"But you look sad," said Emm. "Why are you sad?"

"I am a little sad," said Zuze. "He did not sing the best song. He did not sing 'Susie Girl.' "

Rufus Roth left the stage. It was time for a break. The people in the seats got up. They needed a break too.

"We will wait," said Ms. Cleff. "We will wait for the break to end. There are too many people going to the lobby."

The class stayed by the stage. Zuze

looked for Rufus Roth. But he was gone. Zuze wanted to see him one more time. Maybe she could find him. Maybe she could hear him sing "Susie Girl." She would slip away. She would be fast. She would come right back.

Ms. Cleff watched the people. The kids watched the people. Even Emm watched the people. But Zuze did not watch. Zuze walked away. She walked slowly. She went up onto the stage.

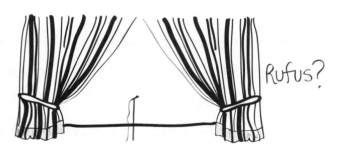

"Where did Rufus Roth go?" Zuze said. She went behind the curtains. She saw a black door. She went through the door. She saw a hall. She walked down the hall. Then she saw a white door. The door had words on it. The words said Rufus Roth. The door was open a little.

Zuze looked back down the hall. She saw no one. So she slipped into the room.

"This is Rufus Roth's dressing room," said Zuze. She looked at one wall. There were pictures on it. There were lots of pictures. Some of the pictures were of Rufus. Zuze looked at all the pictures. Then she heard a noise. Someone was coming. Who was it? Was it Rufus? The door began to open. Zuze got excited.

Then she saw Rufus! He was coming into the room. Zuze was so happy. She couldn't wait to tell Emm. But then something happened. Something really bad happened. Rufus looked at Zuze. He looked right at Zuze. And he looked mad.

"Who are you?" asked Rufus. "And how did you get in here?"

Not invisible? Uh-oh...

1
RUFUS ROTH

Zuze looked behind her. There was no one there. Who was Rufus talking to? Was he talking to her? Could he see her? He should not be able to see her.

Rufus closed the door. "Who are you?" Rufus asked again. "Tell me who you are."

"Um," said Zuze. "Um." She did not know what to say.

"This is my dressing room," said Rufus. "Fans should not come in here."

Zuze had an idea. She would tell Rufus she was a fan. It was true. She was a fan. She would tell him about the class trip.

39

That was true too.

Zuze looked at Rufus. "I am here with my class," said Zuze. "We came to hear you. I'm sorry I came in. I am a big fan. I wanted to meet you."

Rufus walked to a chair. He sat down. He had a glass of water. He had a snack. He looked tired. He needed a break.

Rock Star Time-Out:

"You have to go," said Rufus. "I need a break."

"Okay," said Zuze. "But I want to tell you one thing. I think you are a star. You are the best singer of all time."

Rufus smiled. "You think so?" he asked. Zuze nodded. "Why do you think I am the best?"

"Your songs are great," said Zuze. "Your words are happy. Your music is jumpy. You have a good voice. I love to hear you sing."

"Thank you," said Rufus. He took a drink of water. He ate a bit of his snack. Zuze kept talking.

"I liked your concert," said Zuze. "I liked

41

the songs you sang. But you did not sing your best song."

"Which song is my best song?" he asked.

"I know all your songs," said Zuze. "But the best is 'Susie Girl.' "

Rufus frowned. He shook his head. But Zuze talked some more.

"I like it so much," she said. "I learned all the music. I learned all the words." Rufus sat up in his chair. He looked hard at Zuze.

"Really?" asked Rufus. "You know all the music and words? Will you sing it for me?"

Zuze was excited. She would show Rufus how much she liked his song. She closed her eyes. She began to sing.

Rufus sat very still. He listened to Zuze sing. Rufus began to smile. He got up. Zuze kept singing. He got some music paper and a pencil. As Zuze was singing, Rufus started to write. He wrote very fast. Zuze sang the whole song. Then she opened her eyes.

Rufus stopped writing. He looked at Zuze.

"That was very good," said Rufus. "You sang that really well."

Zuze smiled. "I need to go back to my class now," she said. "They will be looking for me."

"Yes, you should go," said Rufus. "Thank you singing that song so well."

"Thank you for writing it," said Zuze.

Rufus went to the door. He opened the door for her. A man was coming down the hall. He came in Rufus's room. He did not look at Zuze. She slipped out behind the man.

Zuze ran back to the stage. She saw her class. The kids were watching the people sit back down. Ms. Cleff was watching the people too. Zuze joined her class. No one saw her. Then Emm turned around.

"Zuze!" said Emm. "Where were you? I could not see you. I did not tell Ms. Cleff. But I was worried."

"I will tell you," said Zuze. "But you won't believe me!"

8
RUFUS AND ZUZE

Rufus Roth sat in his dressing room. He was still writing on the music paper. The man who came in sat on the couch.

"The first part of your concert was good," said the man. "Are you ready for the next?"

Have a seat.
Act 2 can wait...

"Thanks, Bob," said Rufus. "But I'm not ready yet. Give me a sec." Rufus kept writing lots of notes. He wrote fast. Bob got up. He came over to Rufus. He looked at the music paper.

"What are you doing?" asked Bob. "It's time for the rest of the show. You need to go and sing."

"Not yet," said Rufus again. "I'm almost done. That girl gave me a good idea."

Bob looked around the room. He went to the door. He looked down the hall.

"What girl?" asked Bob. "There's no one here."

"There was a girl in here," said Rufus. "A young girl. She went out the door when you came in."

Bob shook his head. "No one went out the door when I came in," he said. "You were in here all by yourself."

Where did she go?

"She was here," said Rufus. "You just weren't looking. Said her name was Susie. Said she was a fan. She told me I was a star. Then she sang a song. She said it was my

47

best song. It was a sweet song. I'm writing it down now."

"I don't think there was a girl," said Bob again.

"You just didn't see her," said Rufus. He put down his pencil. "Okay. I'm ready now. Let's go finish the concert."

Rufus left his dressing room. He went back on the stage. But Zuze was gone. She was in the lobby with her class. She was talking softly to Emm.

"Are you sure Rufus saw you?" asked Emm. "How can that happen?"

"I don't know," said Zuze. "But he saw me. We talked. And I sang 'Susie Girl' for him."

"But what about rule number two?" asked Emm. She wanted to ask more. But Ms. Cleff started to talk.

"Our trip is over," said Ms. Cleff. "We saw five singers. Now it's time to go back to the TTC. Is everyone ready?"

Ready for time travel

Everyone put away their notepads. Ms. Cleff buzzed Jiff. Zuze closed her eyes. She felt a shake. She felt a wiggle. Then she opened her eyes. She was not in the lobby of a concert hall. She was back in the TTC. The time travel trip was over.

9
FRIENDS?

"Welcome back," said Jiff.

Zuze opened her eyes. The class was back. They were in the big room with the circles on the floor.

"Did you have a good trip?" asked Jiff. He looked at Ms. Cleff.

"We did have a good trip," said Ms. Cleff. "Thank you for your help."

Jiff looked at the class.

"I know this was your first time travel trip," said Jiff. "Does anyone want to ask anything?"

Emm put up her hand. Jiff nodded at her.

"I want to know something," said Emm. "My friend said she—"

Zuze stepped on Emm's foot. She did not want Emm to talk about Rufus Roth. Zuze did not want anyone to know about her and Rufus. Emm stopped talking.

Be quiet, Emm!

"Yes," said Jiff. "What were you saying?"

Emm looked at Zuze. Zuze shook her head. Emm looked back at Jiff.

"Can you remind me about rule number two?" asked Emm.

"Yes, I can," said Jiff. "Rule number two says no one in the past can see or hear you."

RULE #2

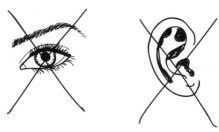

"Is that always true?" asked Emm. "Has anyone ever talked to a person in the past."

Jiff laughed. "No," he said. "That has never happened. It cannot happen. That is not the way time travel works."

"That's what I thought," said Emm. Then she looked at Zuze.

"It did not happen," Emm said softly. "You must have dreamed you talked to Rufus Roth."

Zuze was mad.

"No!" said Zuze. "I did talk to Rufus. And he talked to me. I know what happened."

"I think you made it up," said Emm.

"I did not," said Zuze. Her voice was loud. Ms. Cleff frowned.

"Is something the matter, Zuze?" asked Ms. Cleff.

Zuze shook her head. Then she moved away from Emm. She did not look at her friend.

"It is time to go, class," said Ms. Cleff. "We need to get back to school." Ms. Cleff led the class out of the room.

Zuze walked fast. She did not want to be near Emm. The class went out of the TTC.

They got on the zoom bus. Zuze sat in the back of the bus. Emm sat in the front. The zoom bus flew back to school. Everyone got off.

Emm did not walk with Zuze. Zuze did not walk with Emm. The girls were mad at each other. They were not friends anymore.

not anymore

10
SUSIE GIRL

The kids went to their classroom. It was time to work. It was time to write their papers.

"Okay, class," said Ms. Cleff. "Now you will write your papers. Pick one of the singers. Write about their concert. Use your notes to help you. Also, tell about your singer's life. Use the info net for that."

The kids took out their notes. They took out their computers. Soon Zuze could hear the other kids. They were talking to their computers. The computers were writing their words.

Zuze looked at her computer. What should she write? Should she write about her talk with Rufus? Jiff said it could not happen. Emm said it did not happen. But Zuze did talk to Rufus. Didn't she? Maybe it *was* a dream. Maybe she really didn't talk to Rufus.

Zuze started her paper. She talked to her computer. She talked about Rufus's concert.

"I went to a Rufus Roth concert," said Zuze. "It was the year 2040. Rufus wore white pants and a blue shirt. I heard him sing two songs."

Zuze wrote a good paper. She liked Rufus. She liked the concert. Zuze put a list at the end of the paper. It was a list of all of Rufus's songs. Zuze put a star next to "Susie Girl." It was Rufus's best song. Then Zuze looked on the info net. She wanted dates for each song. She got to "Susie Girl." She stopped. Something was wrong.

"Emm, come here," said Zuze. "Look at this."

Emm came to Zuze's desk.

"What is it?" asked Emm.

"Look at this date," said Zuze. "Rufus wrote 'Susie Girl' in 2041. But how can that be? We visited him in 2040."

"You mean Rufus had not written 'Susie Girl' yet?" asked Emm.

"That's right," said Zuze. She was getting excited. "It was me. I gave him the idea. I'm the one who sang it to him."

"But time travelers can't change the past," said Emm.

"And time travelers can't be seen," said Zuze. "But Rufus saw me."

"Look up more about the song,'" said Emm. "Find out why Rufus wrote it."

Zuze looked on the info net. She looked up "Susie Girl." The two girls read the words. Emm's eyes opened very wide. This is what the words said:

Rufus Roth wrote "Susie Girl" in 2041. Rufus said he got the idea from a fan. She came into his dressing room. She talked to him. Then the girl sang him a song. Rufus never saw the girl again. He wasn't able to thank her for the idea. But "Susie Girl" became his best song. He said he named it after her.

Emm looked at Zuze. "You did talk to Rufus," said Emm. "You really did!"

"Yes," said Zuze. She had a big grin. "I

did talk to Rufus. And I sang to Rufus. Hm. I wonder. Why could he see me?"

"I don't know," Emm said. "We may never know. But we do know one thing."

"We do?" said Zuze. "What's that?"

"We know why Rufus is a star," said Emm. "Because of you!"

SUSIE GIRL

#**1** HIT
SONG by

Rufus
Roth